JOYCE MAXNER

Lady Bugatti

ILLUSTRATED BY KEVIN HAWKES

LOTHROP, LEE & SHEPARD BOOKS   NEW YORK

Library of Congress Cataloging in Publication Data. Maxner, Joyce. Lady Bugatti / by Joyce Maxner ; illustrated
by Kevin Hawkes.   p.   cm.   Summary: Lady Bugatti and her insect guests dine together and then have
an enjoyable evening at the theater. ISBN 0-688-10340-5. — ISBN 0-688-10341-3 (lib. bdg.)   [1. Animals—
Fiction. 2. Stories in rhyme.]   I. Hawkes, Kevin, ill.   II. Title.   PZ8.3.M44935Lad   1991   [E]—dc20
90-19127 CIP AC

for Daryl and John, the words

and music of my life   J.M.

to Mom and Dad   K.H.

Lady Bugatti is having a party
starting tonight at six o'clock.
After we dine she is being so kind
as to give us all tickets for a show down the block.

Bupji Beetle,
Dragonia Fly,
Anatole Ant,
Madame Flutterby,
Bumbly Bee, and you and I
are guests of Lady Bugatti.

Lady Bugatti tinkles a bell
and that means dinner is served.
Two little mice do it beautifully well,
curving their very long tails.

Green turtle soup,
yellow corn mash,
pink radish salad,
red flannel hash,
with blueberry slump for dessert at the last,
and a ginger-ale toast
for our hostess, Lady Bugatti.

Lady Bugatti ruffles her fan
and that means dinner is done.
Two little mice with a brush and a pan
snuff out the candles and sweep up the crumbs.

Bupji Beetle,
Dragonia Fly,
Anatole Ant,
Madame Flutterby,
Bumbly Bee, and you and I
troop out the door in the starry night,
then politely comes Lady Bugatti.

Lady Bugatti waves her muff in the air
and that means the car is coming.
A bright green frog is the perfect chauffeur.
In we climb with the motor humming.

Dragonia perches on Anatole's knees.
Flutterby sits on Bumbly Bee's.
Bupji squeezes
between you and me,
and we drive down the avenue
cozy as peas
to the theater with Lady Bugatti.

Lady Bugatti slips off her gloves.
The show is about to begin.
We are ushered to seats by a gray-feathered dove.
The crowd hushes. The houselights dim.

Bupji Beetle,
Dragonia Fly,
Anatole Ant,
Madame Flutterby,
Bumbly Bee, and you and I
stare at the empty seat on the aisle,
where she ought to be: no Lady Bugatti!

THE MAESTRO LIFTS HIS BATON...THE SHOW MUST GO ON!

Cat MacTavish blows on his trombone.
Rollo Rat tiptoes a high wire.
Piglet Pu hums some songs on her comb.
Mosey Moth leaps through hoops of fire!

An owl croons a love poem to a tree.
Three toads do a tappety-tap.
Shahna Snake ripples up to high C.
Rabbit Jack pulls a bat from a hat.
The theater rings with shouts and cheers
and everyone claps.
But still—no Lady Bugatti.

The last curtain rises before our eyes
and THERE is Lady Bugatti
in her orange gown with black dots all around.
She was in the wings from the start!

She doesn't dance.
She doesn't sing.
As for hoops of fire,
not she!
She is giving the Blue Ribbon Prize
to the owl in love with a tree.
How wonderfully wise!

Bupji Beetle,
Dragonia Fly,
Anatole Ant,
Madame Flutterby,
Bumbly Bee, and you and I
drive away in the grandest style
and THAT means with Lady Bugatti!